ELIZABETH: BOOK THREE

A HORNBOOK CHRISTMAS

ANNE LAUREL CARTER

**Look for the other Elizabeth stories
in Our Canadian Girl**

Book One: Bless This House

Book Two: To Pirate Island

ELIZABETH: BOOK THREE

A HORNBOOK CHRISTMAS

ANNE LAUREL CARTER

PENGUIN
CANADA

PENGUIN CANADA

Published by the Penguin Group

Penguin Group (Canada), 90 Eglinton Avenue East, Suite 700, Toronto, Ontario, Canada M4P 2Y3
(a division of Pearson Penguin Canada Inc.)

Penguin Group (USA) Inc., 375 Hudson Street, New York, New York 10014, U.S.A.
Penguin Books Ltd, 80 Strand, London WC2R 0RL, England
Penguin Ireland, 25 St Stephen's Green, Dublin 2, Ireland (a division of Penguin Books Ltd)
Penguin Group (Australia), 250 Camberwell Road, Camberwell, Victoria 3124, Australia
(a division of Pearson Australia Group Pty Ltd)
Penguin Books India Pvt Ltd, 11 Community Centre, Panchsheel Park, New Delhi – 110 017, India
Penguin Group (NZ), cnr Airborne and Rosedale Roads, Albany, Auckland 1310, New Zealand
(a division of Pearson New Zealand Ltd)
Penguin Books (South Africa) (Pty) Ltd, 24 Sturdee Avenue, Rosebank, Johannesburg 2196,
South Africa

Penguin Books Ltd, Registered Offices: 80 Strand, London WC2R 0RL, England

First published 2005

1 2 3 4 5 6 7 8 9 10   (WEB)

Copyright © Anne Laurel Carter, 2005
Illustrations © Janet Wilson, 2005
Design: Matthews Communications Design Inc.
Map copyright © Sharon Matthews

*Publisher's note: This book is a work of fiction. Names, characters, places, and incidents either
are the product of the author's imagination or are used fictitiously, and any resemblance
to actual persons living or dead, events, or locales is entirely coincidental.*

Manufactured in Canada.

LIBRARY AND ARCHIVES CANADA CATALOGUING IN PUBLICATION

Carter, Anne Laurel, 1953–
Elizabeth : a Hornbook Christmas / Anne Laurel Carter.

(Our Canadian girl)
"Elizabeth: book three".
ISBN 0-14-305011-7

I. Title. II. Title: Hornbook Christmas. III. Series.

PS8555.A7727E44   2005   jC813'.54   C2005-902905-6

Visit the Penguin Group (Canada) website at **www.penguin.ca**

For my mom, who taught me to read

Yukon
Northwest Territories
Nunavut
British Columbia
Alberta
Saskatchewan
Manitoba
Ontar

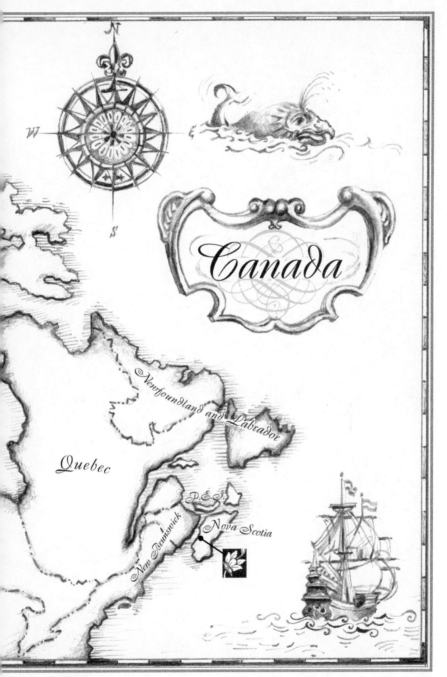

Canada

Newfoundland and Labrador

Quebec

P.E.I.

New Brunswick

Nova Scotia

 Marks the location of the story

ELIZABETH'S STORY CONTINUES

A FTER RESCUING ELIZABETH from Pirate Island, Sarah Worth and Mathilde LeBlanc have finally become friends. The friendship is not encouraged by Sarah's father, Caleb Worth. As the strict and powerful leader of the new Congregationalist community in Nova Scotia, Caleb Worth views all Acadians—who are French and Catholic—as enemies of the English colony. For one hundred and fifty years, the peaceful Acadians had owned this land, but as France and England prepared for war, the Acadians' lands were confiscated and their houses burned. The people were deported and ordered never to come back.

It was Elizabeth's father who had asked that the LeBlanc family be allowed to stay, but at any moment Caleb Worth could ask Captain Mercer at the English fort to put the LeBlancs back in prison. Caleb Worth is a difficult man to like. He is rigid in his views and self-centred as he protects the interests of the English Protestants—his *own* interests. Like other wealthy men in 1762, he sees nothing wrong with owning slaves. In fact, he has brought two, Ginny and her mother, from Connecticut to work as domestic servants in the Worth household.

Sarah's bossiness is inherited, or learned, from her father. It doesn't go away and still annoys Mathilde and Elizabeth. Nevertheless, they've learned to appreciate Sarah's generous heart and openness to others, especially those unlike herself. One friendship in particular, Sarah's fondness for Mathilde's brother Lucien, seems destined to get them all in trouble.

In spite of the conflicts in her world, Elizabeth continues to be excited about life in Nova Scotia: the arrival of winter, the new sleigh, and the baby expected in the spring. When she discovers that Mathilde is hiding a secret, Elizabeth finds something hiding in herself as well: a special talent. All of a sudden, Elizabeth is busy planning something that will help her best friend: a hornbook Christmas.

"Do you like boys?"

Elizabeth leaned close to Mathilde so that their mothers couldn't overhear. The girls' end of the kitchen table was covered with shiny red apples from the cold cellar. They peeled the skins and passed the juicy white fruit to the other end of the table. Their mothers cored and sliced the apples, and then strung thin circles of them to dry in front of the hearth.

Mathilde held up an apple with a black hole and grimaced. "I like boys as much as I like worms."

Elizabeth grinned and kept her knife under the peel to get one long, continuous spiral. "Boys can't be *all* bad. Look how wonderful our papas turned out. They were boys once too."

"Yes! And aunts have stories to tell. Horrible stories. Stories about how they survived our papas when they were boys."

Elizabeth laughed. The long spiral peel bounced and broke. Elizabeth sighed and added it to the scrap pile for the pigs. Then she said, "Have you noticed what happens to Sarah whenever Lucien is around?"

Mathilde's knife hung in the air. "She gets moon eyes and acts sweet as sugar. She's headed for trouble, with her father hating all Acadians the way he does. Why does she fancy my brother anyway? What's wrong with the English boys?"

Elizabeth picked up another apple. It was riddled with worms. She wrinkled up her nose and tossed the fruit on the scrap pile too. "Mama says the change will happen to us to one day soon. We'll get interested in boys and it won't matter what language they speak. They'll speak with … *their eyes,*" she said.

Elizabeth stretched her eyes open as wide as possible. Mathilde copied her, and they stared at each other like full-moon idiots and giggled.

"Any boy looks at me like that and I'm going to live on Pirate Island."

"Me too," Mathilde agreed.

"Of course, a baby brother is different. I don't care what you say, I'm hoping for one."

"And as your friend, I'm praying to every saint in heaven you get a sister."

Still smiling, they attacked the pile of apples, looking for good ones. Elizabeth found a big fat one and edged the knife carefully around it, under the skin. Another long peel dangled onto the table.

"Do you ever miss church?"

Mathilde shook her head energetically. She lowered her voice. "I always fell asleep! We haven't been to church since before the deportation. Now on Sundays, Papa tells us Bible stories. Mama misses the priest and church, but my brothers and I prefer Papa, even if he tells the same few stories over and over."

"You're lucky."

They hadn't kept their voices quiet enough. "Elizabeth!" Mama scolded. She arched her back and shifted on the bench, trying to get comfortable. Being pregnant, she appeared to have a big bowl stuck under her dress.

"Mathilde!" Madame LeBlanc joined in. "Is a terrible thing to live without a church."

Mothers had the worst habit of listening to private conversations.

Elizabeth gave Mathilde a silencing glance. The fire crackled and the knives sliced. Soon their mothers' chatter began again. The big kitchen was filled with the smells of their morning's work. Another string of sliced apples was hung before the great opening of the hearth.

Outside it was a cold November morning, but inside the kitchen, it was as warm as a summer's day. The only clue that winter had arrived was the frost covering the windowpanes.

Elizabeth stared at Mathilde in surprise as she realized something. "Can your papa read in English? I could lend him our Bible. Then you'd always have a new story."

A wistful look came over Mathilde's face. She peeked at her mother. There was nothing to fear. She was in the middle of reciting a long, complicated recipe.

"I don't think my papa can read," she whispered. "We have a French Bible but I'm not sure he reads it. Oh, he holds it in front of him and turns the pages but"—her black eyes had a question—"the same story changes every time he tells it. Sometimes it's five loaves and two fish, and other times it's one loaf and six fish." Mathilde paused. Her head tilted to one side. It wasn't like her to be so hesitant. "When you read—doesn't a story always say the same thing?" she asked.

"Yes, but it's easy to make mistakes, especially if you don't practise much."

Elizabeth suddenly realized that she'd never seen Mathilde read. Elizabeth had been the one to read *Robinson Crusoe* to her last summer. And the treasure that Elizabeth had found on Pirate Island, the buried French books that she'd given to Mathilde? She'd never seen Mathilde read those either.

Before she could ask about it, Sarah and Rebecca Worth bustled into the warm kitchen, shaking fresh snow from their shawls.

Elizabeth jumped up and ran to look out the door. "It's snowing!" she cried with excitement. "As soon as there's enough snow, we'll go for a sleigh ride. My father's almost finished our new sleigh."

"You seem more excited to see the snow than you are to see us!" Sarah said with a pout.

"Elizabeth—the door! Your mama needs to stay warm!" Madame LeBlanc scolded.

Elizabeth shut the door quickly and attended to their visitors. "Of course we're glad to see you," she said. "Look at all the apples we're drying. You can lend a hand. Doesn't it smell good in here?" She took the heavy shawls from Sarah and her mother and hung them up.

Sarah was dressed in Sunday finery even though it was mid-week.

"Like my new dress?" she said, twirling around for Elizabeth to admire it.

"Now, Sarah, I warned you about showing off," her mother said, going to sit with the other women.

Elizabeth nodded—how could she say no?—and stared at the drawstring waist and fancy tucks of Sarah's silk dress. It was deep blue and must have cost more than all the dresses that she and Mama had ever owned between them. She caught Mathilde staring too. Only a month ago, Mathilde would have resented Sarah's wealth and her father's growing success as a shipbuilder. But just before All Saints' Eve, Sarah had helped Mathilde rescue Elizabeth from Pirate Island. And Sarah had arranged a paying job for Mathilde at her uncle's house. Mr. Porter's wife had died and he needed help with his little boy, Joshua. After all that, Mathilde had put aside her pride and had seen Sarah's good points, although she liked to grumble, "Sometimes, they're hard to find."

"We just have to finish these apples and then we can go outside to chop wood," Elizabeth said. "Want to help?"

"Chop wood? Peel apples? *In this dress?*" Sarah stayed several steps away from the sticky mess on the table. "It's silk from China. Papa had it made …" she paused for effect, "for my thirteenth birthday."

"You'll look more beautiful with an axe in your hand," Mathilde said, a glint in her eye. "I think Lucien's outside, needing help."

Sarah looked out the window. "Is he? I didn't see him."

Mathilde nudged Elizabeth.

Sarah noticed the nudge. "Stop teasing me. I want you both to feel how much lighter silk is than homespun. Oh, mind, not if your hands are sticky."

"I'll just wipe them on your skirt." Mathilde reached out both hands. Sarah half-screamed, half-laughed, and took another step back.

Elizabeth laughed at the good-natured teasing. "Let's see who you shall marry in that grand dress of yours." She licked her fingers clean and wiped them on a towel. She held up the longest apple peel by one end, allowing it to uncoil in the air. "Come close and turn your back. Don't be such a powder puff. I won't let it touch your precious dress."

Sarah turned and leaned back as Elizabeth hung the peel carefully down one deep-blue-covered shoulder blade.

"Mathilde," Sarah cried. "Do tell me what letter's on my back."

"I can't."

"What do you mean you can't? Just read the shape of the letter. Can't you read?"

Mathilde muttered something. Her arms were crossed and her eyes were small and angry. What was wrong? Had Mathilde never played the game of trying to find a letter shape in a fruit peel? Was it because Sarah was making such a fuss about her new dress? Or did Mathilde really not know what the letter was? If there was one thing Elizabeth had learned about Mathilde over the last seven months, it was not to embarrass her in front of others.

"*I'll* tell you what it is. Let's see ..."

With her free hand, Elizabeth showed as tactfully as possible how the peel dropped straight down and curled to the right. "It's an *L*. Too bad for Sarah. I can't think of anyone in Nova Scotia whose name starts with *L*. Can you, Mathilde?"

Mathilde's eyes looked like two pieces of coal. She shook her head, refusing to speak. Elizabeth pretended nothing was wrong.

"Poor Sarah. I've thought of someone. Governor Lawrence. He's terribly old."

"And terribly dead!" Sarah laughed, turning around to face them. "So it can't be him. It has to be someone alive. Someone young. Someone like—"

Sarah stopped herself just in time. The mothers were listening. Her mother and Mathilde's mother both had the same look of dread on their

*Sarah turned and leaned back
as Elizabeth hung the peel
carefully down one deep-blue-
covered shoulder blade.*

faces. Everyone in the room knew that Sarah liked Lucien LeBlanc. But Lucien and his family were under the watchful eye of Captain Mercer, who was stationed at the English fort, and Caleb Worth had threatened to have Lucien sent to prison in Halifax if Sarah was ever seen speaking to him again.

Elizabeth's mother rescued the situation. "Someone like Luke Driscoll? What a nice young man he is. So like his father, don't you think, Rebecca?"

Mrs. Worth nodded, but the near-mention of Lucien's name and the fear of Caleb Worth's wrath had brought a chill into the kitchen. They worked silently. The only sounds were the ones made by their peeling and slicing and, every now and then, the thump of the corer against the wooden cutting board.

Soon the mothers began to talk again, sharing apple recipes. Elizabeth didn't listen. She was too lost in thought, remembering how she'd given Mathilde the books that she'd found buried on

Pirate Island. For more than a month now, they hadn't read them. Mathilde had made up all manner of excuses, but now Elizabeth guessed the real reason.

Mathilde couldn't read and was embarrassed about it. And Sarah, typical Sarah, had made it impossible for Mathilde to admit it.

Elizabeth smiled, remembering how her mother had taught her to read. Maybe, if she planned it carefully, Elizabeth could do the same for her friend. Winter was the perfect season for a school!

CHAPTER № 2

December began with a big snowstorm.
Dreaming how she'd run the first home school in
Nova Scotia, Elizabeth watched every flake from
her bedroom window. There were thousands, no
millions of them! She'd have to teach a little
arithmetic along with reading and writing, the
way Mama had taught her and several other children back in Connecticut.

What if Mama wanted to take over? She
loved Mama, but *she* wanted to be the teacher.
Best not to say anything. But how could she
teach reading without supplies? She'd *have* to

ask Mama; it was so frustrating!

In the afternoon, she found a way to ask Mama.

"Did we bring the hornbooks with us?" Elizabeth asked, sweeping up the cold ashes in the hearth for soap-making.

"What's the matter with me?" Mama exclaimed. "I meant to start a school when we finished with the harvest and here it is, past your birthday, almost Christmas."

"So we *did* bring them?"

"I'm sure I packed them in the trunk with my wedding dress." She gave Elizabeth a teasing smile. "You never know when these things might come in handy again."

"Could I check?"

"Right now?"

It didn't take much begging before Elizabeth was rummaging through Mama's trunk. She found several hornbooks and brought them to the kitchen table. There was also a slate board edged with wood and four slate pencils wrapped in paper.

"It's how you taught me to read, isn't it? You started with the alphabet and then ... and then what?"

"What's on your mind, Elizabeth? Out with it."

Should she hide it from Mama? After all the trouble she'd caused over Pirate Island, Elizabeth couldn't bear the thought of deceiving her mother now. "I want to start a little school. Maybe start with ..." She was reluctant to say Mathilde's name—no one must know her secret— so instead she said, "Joshua Porter. Seeing how he lost his mother and he's turned five, isn't it time he learns his letters?"

There she'd said it. Her plan was almost out in the open. She eyed Mama carefully. Mama was busy mixing the ashes and lard.

"I don't think that's possible right now."

Elizabeth felt as if someone were pouring ashes onto her dream, but then Mama sighed. "I have so much to do to get ready for Christmas and then for the baby. All the clothes and furniture to make. And Papa and I still have to assemble the loom."

Mama must have sensed Elizabeth's disappointment because she added, almost as an afterthought, "But maybe you could find someone else to teach in my place for an hour or two in the afternoons. I just don't think I have time for it now."

Elizabeth was so excited that she nearly dropped the broom. "I do know someone," she cried. "Me!"

Mama laughed. "I know you're eleven, but you'd be the youngest teacher in Nova Scotia. And the first!" Mama added as tactfully as possible, "Are you sure you know how to plan a lesson?"

Elizabeth wasn't about to admit that she didn't have even a glimmering of an idea. "I remember everything, and I have some ideas of my own I'd like to try. I could teach him his letters when Matilde's working there."

Her mother nodded, hiding a smile. "I used to think you took after your father. But maybe you have a calling for teaching as I did and my mother before me. You'll do a fine job. If you'll take a word of advice, you'd do well to find at least another student or two. Joshua will learn better in a little group."

Elizabeth nodded. "They don't have to be the same age, do they?"

"No. Big ones help the little ones—and you'll be surprised how quickly the little ones learn. Which reminds me: Maggie and Priscilla Young never learned back in Connecticut. They lived too far from our house, remember? They might be interested in your school."

Elizabeth's dream was so close that she could almost hear the scratchy sound of a slate pencil on a slate board. But something warned her that she should see how things went with Joshua and Mathilde first.

"I'd love to have more students, Mama. But I'd rather practise with Joshua first. Wait until I'm sure of what I'm doing."

"Why, Elizabeth Brightman, how very wise of you."

Elizabeth blushed. She couldn't tell her mother the real reason for her caution—not yet. She piled the teaching materials into a basket, her mind racing with plans. She'd start teaching Mathilde tomorrow! All her worrying had been for nothing.

CHAPTER № 3

The snowstorm ended and when Mathilde dropped by on the way to work the next afternoon, Elizabeth took the first careful step toward achieving her goal. She asked to come along to the Porters' house, without mentioning a school. "I need something to do. I could bring dried apples and make an apple cobbler for Joshua and his father."

Mathilde laughed. "If you can keep Joshua busy for a half-hour, I may get some washing done. He's always into something."

Mathilde had her hands full keeping the house

clean and minding Joshua. Mr. Porter went to the shipyard in the afternoon, where he worked for Caleb Worth.

Just then, Papa opened the front door. The sudden draft of cold air made Elizabeth shiver. "Would you girls like a ride in the new sleigh? It's ready for its first passengers."

Elizabeth and Mathilde nodded with excitement. Sleigh rides were the best part of winter.

"Could you take us to the Porters' house?" Elizabeth asked, pulling her heavy coat from its hook.

"Sure thing. But first we'll stop at Fort Edward. Matthew Young told me that some Mi'kmaq are trading furs there, and we could use a heavy bearskin for the sleigh," Papa said.

The girls bundled up and joined Papa in the sleigh. He stood behind them on a platform holding the reins to the oxen in front. It was a bright, sunny afternoon. The runners under the sleigh slid through the sparkling snow as the oxen plodded steadily up the hill. Elizabeth imagined they were a very slow comet, burning across the land while a million stars twinkled around them.

English soldiers guarding the open wooden gates nodded to them as they entered the fort. The Acadian prisoners who had repaired the dykes and helped with the harvest had been sent to Halifax, and it seemed unusually quiet inside the fort. Only a few Mi'kmaq men stood beside their piles of furs. Elizabeth stared at them nervously before she climbed from the sleigh. She'd heard that the Mi'kmaq had made a winter settlement not far up the bay, but this was the first time she'd seen them so close. Tobacco pipes hung from their mouths. Their jackets were embroidered and open at the neck, showing bright tattoos of crosses and suns on their dark chests. Their faces were stern and expressionless; she stayed close to Papa.

Mathilde, however, jumped down and ran toward them as if they were old friends.

"*Nikmaq!*" she cried.

The men's faces changed completely. They smiled broadly and held out their hands to her. *"Nikmaq!"* they cried back.

Elizabeth watched in amazement as Mathilde chattered away and they replied. Papa unloaded a large bag of flour and oats, and he smiled at the men too. What had she been so afraid of?

"Well, Mathilde. Would you be my interpreter? Could you ask if there's a big bearskin to trade for these?"

In no time everyone was nodding, satisfied with their trade, and Elizabeth was back in the sleigh beside Mathilde, tucked snugly under the bearskin. It was so warm and cozy that she was sure they could ride all the way back to Connecticut and never feel the cold.

Elizabeth remembered the scene in the fort and turned to Mathilde. "What did you say to them? That first word that made them smile?"

"Nikmaq."

"What's it mean?"

Mathilde scrunched up her face. "I'm not sure.

It's what we always said when we met. I think it's something like *my brothers.*"

"Are they really your brothers?"

Mathilde laughed. "You know who my brothers are!"

"But you weren't afraid of them?"

"Afraid of them?" Mathilde's black eyes were wide with amazement. "One of my aunts is Mi'kmaq. They were friends to Acadians. They shared everything. The land. Their stories. And they had the best feasts in the summer. I remember those. There were races and games and so much food."

Elizabeth was quiet all the way to the Porters' house. She envied Mathilde's good memories. She loved Nova Scotia just the way it was, yet it was strange to think it had been a far different place for Mathilde only a few years earlier.

In front of the Porters' house, Papa called for the oxen to stop and pulled on the reins.

"I'll be back for you girls before dark."

The girls jumped out and dashed up the beaten path to the open front door where Joshua and his father stood waiting. Joshua announced proudly, "I saw you from the window. I helped Papa milk the cows. There's lots of cream on top for you to make butter."

Elizabeth felt her heart flip-flop. How would Mathilde ever join the first lesson if she had to work all afternoon?

Though he seemed surprised to see her, Mr. Porter nodded in a welcoming way and then put on his coat. Since his wife's death in October, Elizabeth hadn't heard the man speak to anyone. He only nodded. She hoped that he spoke to Joshua. She mustered up her courage to say, "Mr. Porter, sir, I've come with some apples … and my mother's school supplies. Would you like me to teach Joshua to read?"

She kept her eyes on Mr. Porter but was aware of Mathilde turning to stare at her. Mr. Porter nodded and left. So far so good.

"I'm going to read?" Joshua asked, clapping his

hands. "Like Mama? From a book? Today?"

"Yes, Joshua. But we don't start with a book. And it won't happen all at once. It takes a long time. If you like, we can have school lessons and you'll learn."

"No books?"

Mathilde interrupted. Her voice was sarcastic. "Where's the cream, Joshua?" she called. "I can't do this all by myself."

Joshua ran to the back of the kitchen, picked up a pail, and struggled to carry it over to Mathilde. She took it from him, grumbling, "All right. Enough. You have more important things to do."

Mathilde wouldn't look at Elizabeth. By the way that Mathilde slopped the cream into the churner, Elizabeth knew that her friend was mad.

"What if I set up a little school for Joshua—it would keep him out from under your feet? What do you think?"

"Go right ahead. Only I thought you were going to make apple cobbler. That's at least something you could finish in a day."

Mathilde's movements were sharp and energetic. She pounded the thrasher as if a dangerous animal were trapped inside the butter churner. She was going to ruin the butter if she didn't calm down.

This was not going to be as easy as Elizabeth had hoped. She said a little prayer. *If Mathilde wants to learn to read, please tell her that this would be a good time to start.*

Nervously, Elizabeth pulled a hornbook from her basket and placed it on the kitchen table in front of Joshua. The first lesson was not off to a good start.

"What's this?" Joshua asked. He picked up the hornbook and peered at it as if it were a mirror.

"It's called a hornbook."

"It doesn't look like a horn. It looks like a paddle."

"All those black marks at the top are the letters of the alphabet. See? And that's the Lord's Prayer at the bottom. And it's covered with a thin piece of horn to protect it. It's for learning your letters. When you've learned all the letters of the alphabet, you'll own the keys to a great kingdom. The kingdom of reading."

All Joshua could say was a big "Ohhh."

The thrashing in the butter churning suddenly calmed down. Elizabeth didn't dare look at Mathilde. Was she tired? Or listening?

Elizabeth pulled a tiny book from her basket. It was covered in pretty Dutch flowery paper and fit into the palm of her hand. She showed Joshua the first page.

"This is called the Royal Primer. My mother used this to teach us to read in Connecticut. The first page has a funny verse you'll never forget."

The butter churning stopped completely as Elizabeth read:

He who ne'er learns his A, B, C
For ever will a blockhead be;
But he who to his books inclin'd
Will soon a golden treasure find.

Joshua shook his head. "I don't want to be a blockhead."

Elizabeth laughed. "You won't be when we're through. Let me get a fescue and I'll say the names of all the letters as I point to them. We'll start with the small letters."

She closed the Royal Primer and pulled a shaped bone as long as her hand from the basket. Pointing the sharp tip of the fescue at the hornbook, she said the name of each letter carefully.

To her dismay, Joshua's eyes glazed over. Elizabeth panicked. Maybe twenty-six letters were too many? Could she make this easier for him? And fun? Then she remembered "The Alphabet Song." She sang it slowly several times, and each time she reached the end, "Now we shall begin again …," she hoped that Joshua would try to sing along.

Joshua listened, swung his feet, and smiled, but he didn't join in. Elizabeth stopped singing. This teaching was hard work. What had Mama done? What should she try next?

Slowly, she sang just the first phrase of the song, *"A, B, C, D,"* pointing at the letters.

Joshua brightened and sang it back to her. Success!

She continued on this way, breaking the song into short bits. Mathilde kept her back to them, quietly churning the butter. She had to be listening. She was churning the butter in rhythm to the alphabet. And there, faintly, wasn't that the sound of Mathilde's voice singing along?

"Good, Joshua. Now you have one more thing to learn today and I think that will be enough. You might as well learn to read and write together. Then when we're done with our school, at the end of winter, you'll be able to write some words."

"Will I be able to write Mama a letter?"

The question startled Elizabeth. She pulled a slate board and pencil from her basket. How would they send a letter to Heaven? Without knowing the answer, she nodded. "Of course you will. Today you'll learn to make the first letter. Small *a* is shaped like an apple with a knife beside it, ready to cut."

She drew the letter on the board.

Immediately, Mathilde stopped churning the butter and brought a rag and vinegar to clean the window behind them. Elizabeth bent her head so that Mathilde could watch if she wanted to, unnoticed.

"Would you like to try?" Elizabeth asked, giving Joshua the slate pencil.

Joshua made several letters, each one better than the last.

"That's excellent, Joshua. Now you know the first letter. *A* is for *aaa*pple." She exaggerated the beginning vowel sound.

"Can I try too?"

Mathilde had stopped cleaning the window and was leaning over the table, watching the magic on the slate board.

Joshua gave her the pencil happily. "Your turn."

With the rag, Mathilde wiped off Joshua's letters and made her own. Her face was intense with concentration.

Elizabeth was so hopeful, she was afraid to say anything.

"That was too easy," Mathilde said. "Show us more. What were the next ones in your song?" She looked at the hornbook and sang. *"A, B, C, D, E—"*

"Stop!" Elizabeth laughed. "We can't do them all in one day. We'll do two more today and maybe three more tomorrow."

She picked up the slate pencil and demonstrated. "Here's *b* for butter and *c* for cobbler."

In no time at all, Mathilde and Joshua had mastered the first three letters and the sounds they made.

The light was growing dimmer in the kitchen. Mathilde didn't want to light a precious candle but agreed they could light a lantern. "It's gotten so late," Mathilde groaned. "I must get back to work or nothing will be ready for Joshua's papa and he won't let us have school tomorrow."

Elizabeth's heart skipped. Mathilde had said "us." Elizabeth pulled out another of Mama's hornbooks from the basket and held it out to her friend. "I wasn't sure if you'd want me to teach you."

For the teeniest second, Mathilde's chest puffed up with pride. Elizabeth wished she'd said nothing. But then Mathilde's eyes began to dance.

"Oh, what's the use pretending?" she said, throwing up her hands. "I can't read. None of us can." She shook her finger at Elizabeth. "The priest ran a school during the winter and my brothers were about to go, but we were deported. How I'd love to show them I can do something they can't. I'm going to read. They'll be the blockheads!" she crowed.

Elizabeth cheered for Mathilde. "Lucien won't shoo us away like flies any more. Wait till we tell him that you're learning to read!"

A look of panic crossed Mathilde's face. "Don't tell. Not yet. Please, Elizabeth. I can't read yet. Not even the treasure you found on Pirate Island. All I know is what you taught us today. *A, B, C.* They'll laugh at me if that's all I know."

Elizabeth nodded. "It will be our secret."

They both turned to stare at Joshua at the same moment.

Mathilde bent down face to face with him. "Can you keep this a secret? Don't tell anyone I'm learning to read with you."

Joshua nodded seriously. "I love secrets."

Elizabeth had a sinking feeling that five-year-olds could hold secrets as well as a leaky boat could hold water, but she said nothing to ruin Mathilde's excitement. Besides, they had too much work to do to worry. Quickly, they threw themselves into finishing the butter and making an apple cobbler. Elizabeth insisted that Joshua count the apple slices out loud—how could she call herself a teacher and not have an arithmetic lesson? She showed him the numbers at the bottom of his hornbook. Then she helped Mathilde tidy the kitchen. Together they swept out the old ashes in the hearth and saved them in a bucket. They were out of soap to wash the dirty clothes. They would have to wait for another day. They built up the fire and cut chunks of meat and vegetables to begin a stew that would last a few days.

Before they knew it, Joshua's papa was back from the shipyard. Elizabeth was tired, but her heart was happy. The Porters' house was full of good smells and satisfied smiles—though Mr. Porter merely nodded at them before they ran out and climbed into Papa's waiting sleigh.

"*A, B, C!*" Joshua yelled, waving goodbye.

"*C* is for cobbler!" Mathilde called back.

Under the bearskin blanket, Elizabeth hugged her basket of school supplies close to her chest. With the sun already set, the air had grown even colder. Inside she was ablaze with ideas for the next lesson. She couldn't wait to see Mama and tell her about the first day of school. She'd keep the part about Mathilde to herself, but she had an uneasy feeling Mathilde's secret wouldn't be a secret for long.

CHAPTER No 5

Elizabeth was just beginning her second lesson at the Porters' house the next day when the kitchen door opened. Afternoon sunshine flooded the dim room but so did a gust of cold wind; it made the flames in the hearth quiver and Elizabeth shiver.

"Shut the door, quick, and come in," Mathilde yelled, lifting her eyes briefly from her hornbook.

Ginny, the Worths' household slave, stood at the door holding out a big jug.

"Mistress sent me with soft soap. She say she don't want to see Joshua in dirty pants at Sunday

38

Meeting one more time."

"You tell her to mind her own business," Mathilde said, not looking up.

Ginny slammed the door shut and hung her shawl on the hook. "She also say if you all too busy, I'm to do it and I'm to get your wages."

A smile played around Ginny's eyes as she continued. "I sure can use a penny if you all can't. Mama and me been waitin' for years on a certain promise to get our freedom. Mama says if Master Worth don't grant it, we may jess have to save our pennies an' buy it."

Mathilde slammed the hornbook down on the table.

"Those Worths. Always ordering everybody around. I'd like to see Rebecca Worth scrub a kettle of dirty clothes clean. I don't know how you stand it."

Ginny's eyebrows went straight up. She glanced at Joshua to make sure he wasn't listening. He was busy finding *a*'s on his hornbook with his fescue.

"Don't have much choice, do I?" she whispered. "You don't like cleaning them clothes, but you be free."

Mathilde's face changed completely. She went over to Ginny, took the jug with one hand, and slipped the other around Ginny's waist. "I'm sorry, Ginny. I should be thanking you instead of complaining. It's been too cold to make soap outside and Mr. Porter's all out, though I've saved two buckets of ashes already."

Elizabeth felt a prick of jealousy. Mathilde and Ginny had become friends in the last month. Mrs. Worth had sent Ginny to help Mr. Porter almost every day since his wife had died. Ginny rolled up her sleeves and took a big kettle from the fire. She poured steaming water into a huge iron cauldron on the floor as Mathilde added some soap. Without a word, Ginny picked up a wooden paddle and began to stir as Mathilde threw in the dirty clothes.

"Can I help?" Elizabeth asked, wanting to join them.

"No. You'd best teach Joshua the next letter. I'll listen from here."

With a sigh, Elizabeth tapped Joshua on the shoulder. "Time for the letter *d*. It comes after *c*. Can you show me on your hornbook?"

Ginny stopped stirring and let Mathilde take a turn. "What's a hornbook?" she asked shyly.

Elizabeth explained while Joshua pointed out all the *d*'s with his fescue, oblivious to the girls.

"Go on. Take a close look," Mathilde said.

Ginny's face was full of curiosity.

Elizabeth pulled another hornbook from the basket. "Would you like to learn to read, too?"

"I don't rightly know. Mama said it weren't allowed in the South. But Master Worth ain't so mean-spirited as those old cotton masters."

Ginny shook her head but nevertheless came and sat at the table opposite Joshua. She looked at the hornbook skeptically. "That little paddle will teach a body to read?"

Elizabeth pulled out the Royal Primer and read the verse about learning the *A, B, C's*.

"You don't want to be a blockhead, do you, Ginny?" Mathilde laughed.

Ginny shook her head, which made her two thick braids fly about her shoulders. Mathilde dropped the paddle, left the clothes, and sat beside Joshua too.

"Me neither. Those clothes can sit there and clean themselves. I'm not missing school."

"We'll help you with the chores after. Like yesterday," Elizabeth said. "School is better with more students. Mama said so."

She put the hornbook in front of Mathilde, but the empty table in front of Ginny bothered her. She pulled out another hornbook and fescue and placed them in front of Ginny.

Ginny looked troubled. "I gotta ask Master Worth. Mama said they'd lose an ear down south if they was ever caught reading."

Elizabeth and Mathilde gasped together. "That's too horrible," Mathilde said.

Elizabeth remembered how terrifying Caleb Worth had been when he'd found out that his daughter, Sarah, had been walking with Lucien. "I wouldn't want you to get into trouble. Caleb Worth is—"

"Uncle Caleb?" Joshua repeated like a parrot. "What's my Uncle Caleb?"

Nervous looks passed among the girls. Elizabeth was glad that she hadn't finished her sentence. How awful it would be if she said anything thoughtless that got Ginny in trouble.

"He be my Master," Ginny said stiffly. But her chin was up. She picked up the hornbook and waved it as if she were shooing flies. "You all pay attention to your lesson. I'm gonna sit here a spell, rest my bones, like my mama say. Don't mind me. I know just the right words to say to ole Uncle Caleb when I get home."

CHAPTER N.° 6

In the early morning, Elizabeth rushed through her chores in the barn. While she milked Bessie, she chanted with excitement, "I'm a *teacher, teacher, teacher!*"

Bessie twitched her ears and lifted her back foot in a threatening way as if to say, *Enough, enough, enough!*

"Sorry, Bessie." Elizabeth slowed her rhythmic pulls. "Wait till you hear what's happening. I have two students, maybe three. And Mathilde wants to finish the whole alphabet today. But Joshua's mind will wander if we try to do too much.

Teaching's so much harder than I thought."

That afternoon at the Porters', much to Elizabeth's dismay, a surprise visitor solved the problem.

Ginny arrived with Sarah Worth. Elizabeth's smile froze. They were right in the middle of their lesson.

"What are *you* doing here?" Mathilde put her hornbook behind her back and glared at Sarah.

Elizabeth wondered the same thing, but after all they'd been through to become friends, Elizabeth cringed at the return of Mathilde's rudeness.

"I hear there's a school," Sarah said, shaking out the flounces in her skirt, oblivious to Mathilde's tone. "I came to help."

"Oh, no!" Mathilde wailed, throwing the hornbook on the table.

Sarah looked hurt. "Whatever kind of greeting is that?"

"It's supposed to be a secret!" She glared at Joshua, then Ginny. "Who told?"

"Not me," Joshua piped up.

Sarah frowned. "Can't you read?"

Bewildered, Mathilde looked to Ginny for an explanation.

"I never said nothin' about you. I done asked Master Porter if I might learn to read the Bible with Joshua this afternoon. Miss Sarah invited herself along."

Elizabeth nearly laughed out loud. Ginny *had* known just the right words for Caleb Worth.

"I'm sure if you'd stop blabbing about it, your secret would be safe with us," Sarah said. "I've always wanted to be a teacher."

Elizabeth stopped smiling. She wanted to wail. "We don't need another teacher, Sarah. *I'm* the teacher. There are only three students."

Sarah went over to the table and picked up Elizabeth's hornbook. "I have my old one at the house. I can get Ginny caught up tonight. You go right ahead with your lesson today so I can see where you are. I won't be in the way."

Elizabeth wished that Sarah hadn't come. And she wished that she didn't wish it. But they had to continue. They only had an hour left for a lesson.

Mathilde had brought one of her French books, and after Elizabeth had demonstrated the next three letters, Mathilde opened it.

"I want to compare the English and French letters."

Immediately, Sarah jumped up and moved behind Joshua. "Perfect. Elizabeth, you help Mathilde and I'll help Joshua and Ginny. No sense me being idle. After all, I'm two years older than you and know the most."

Elizabeth ground her teeth. She wished that she could be like Bessie this morning and threaten to kick Sarah Worth—kick her out of her school! It was a nasty thought, and she felt horrible for thinking it.

Elizabeth forced herself to sound out, as best she could, a few of the strange words in Mathilde's book, pointing at them with her fescue.

Mathilde giggled. "You make them sound so funny. Like gobbledegook."

Elizabeth stopped and threw down the fescue, totally annoyed at Mathilde now. Her school was ruined. Ruined!

"Most of the letters are the same," Mathilde said. With her head bent over her treasure, she didn't notice Elizabeth's distress. "But see this *e* here and this *a*? They each have a little mark over them. What do they mean?"

"I don't know," Elizabeth huffed. "Ask Sarah."

Mathilde lifted her head quickly and studied Elizabeth. Then she stared at Sarah, who was busy telling Ginny how to make her first letters. Mathilde's eyes narrowed and she nodded her head as if understanding something.

Elizabeth felt Mathilde's warm hand cover hers. A few tears filled Elizabeth's eyes.

Mathilde whispered, "*You* are my teacher. You guessed that I wanted to learn to read my French books."

Immediately, Elizabeth remembered why she'd started the school in the first place. It wasn't for Joshua or Ginny or herself. It was for Mathilde.

Elizabeth felt Mathilde's warm hand cover hers. A few tears filled Elizabeth's eyes.

She squeezed her friend's hand and placed the Royal Primer and the hornbook beside Mathilde's book.

"Those marks are like a riddle. We're going to have to solve what they mean like a riddle."

Elizabeth wrote them on the slate board. If she could figure this riddle out for Mathilde, she'd have the key to her treasure. Suddenly, Elizabeth had an idea.

"Those marks are over vowels."

"What are vowels?"

The hour sped by as Elizabeth showed Mathilde English vowels, consonants, and syllables. She looked over to see Joshua drawing pictures on his slate board and Ginny practising the alphabet with Sarah. The kitchen was too dim to study any more.

"It's time to stop," Elizabeth announced briskly, putting the reading materials back in her basket. "Mathilde has to do her chores now before Joshua's papa gets home."

Sarah pouted. "That doesn't mean *we* have to stop."

"Oh, yes, it does. School's dismissed." Elizabeth packed up their materials too and placed the basket by the front door. The message was only too obvious.

Mathilde put some lard in a few lanterns but didn't light them, waiting for a signal from Elizabeth.

Ginny stood up reluctantly. "I'd best be heading back to the house. I got all your dresses to iron, Miss Sarah."

Sarah left with Ginny and when the door closed behind them, the tension left the room. Joshua was happy to fetch water. Mathilde lit the lanterns and they set to scrubbing, working silently until their hands were raw and the pots were clean.

Finally, Elizabeth's papa arrived to take them home and they sat together under the bearskin rug in the sleigh. It was that wintery time of day just after the sun had set. Everything was silvery—the snow, the trees, even Pirate Island out on the bay. It would last only a few moments before darkness descended and the first stars appeared.

Standing behind her, Papa sang a Christmas carol, his breath hanging in a white fog over her head. Christmas would come soon, then New Year's. Too many good things to let a conflict with Sarah make her unhappy. She could hardly tell Sarah to stay away.

The Christmas carol made her think about forgiveness, which made her think about the Bible, which made her think about …

"I've got it!" she cried.

"What?" Mathilde said.

"How to solve the riddle of the French vowels. Your Bible is in French, isn't it? Bring it to my house after supper. I have a feeling the Gospel of Matthew will help us figure it out."

After supper Mathilde came over with her family Bible. Her mother came too, wanting to help Mama make a little quilt for the new cradle.

Madame LeBlanc set the little wooden bed rocking before she sat down. "You know we like to make a *crèche* for Noël? Christmas Eve? Is a big time for us. I make *rappie* pie with meat and potatoes. And *tarte au sucre*. So many good things to eat. We say prayers at midnight, then we eat. Maybe this year … we feast together?"

Elizabeth listened hopefully and nudged Mathilde. A midnight feast with the LeBlancs on

Christmas Eve—what could be better? Mama looked up from the sea of old cotton spread over the table.

"What's a *crèche,* Mireille?" she asked.

Mireille paused, searching for the right English words. "Baby Jesus, Mary, and Joseph. The animals. The *crèche* reminds us of the story of his birth."

Mama smiled. "Oh, yes. We do the same thing sometimes. Why don't we celebrate here and use our cradle? We'll make a real nativity scene."

The mothers bent their heads over their sewing and chatted about Christmas plans. Mathilde and Elizabeth tiptoed into the hallway and up the stairs with two lanterns, their family Bibles, and the school basket.

"It's still a secret." Mathilde giggled.

Quietly, Elizabeth closed the door to her room, and they sat on the cold wooden planks. "Don't worry. They're busy, but I'll whisper just in case. Listen to this." Elizabeth put the Bibles and the hornbook under the light of the lanterns. She pointed to the bottom of the horn-book and read the Lord's Prayer.

"Do you know this prayer?" she asked Mathilde.

Mathilde nodded. "Of course. Only in French."

"I thought so. It's written in the Bible. So it must be in yours too. Now do you see?" Elizabeth asked, barely able to contain her growing excitement.

Mathilde shook her head, not seeing at all.

Elizabeth flipped through her Bible and found Matthew 6:9, where the Lord's Prayer began. "Quick. Give me yours and I'll see if I can find it."

The Gospel names were similar enough in the two Bibles to find the same passage.

"Now recite the first words slowly, very slowly, and I'll point to each word as you say it. See? Those same funny markings are there over the vowels. We're going to figure out the riddle of the sounds they make."

Mathilde gasped with understanding and began to recite in French, word by word, slowly.

Elizabeth listened hard to what Mathilde said while looking at the words in French.

"They match exactly!" she said triumphantly. "Now let's make a list of the French vowels and the sounds they make."

On a piece of Papa's good stationery paper, Elizabeth copied the French version of the Lord's Prayer. Then she and Mathilde figured out as many vowel sounds as they could from those words. Elizabeth wrote them carefully at the bottom. Then she remembered something Mama used to do with her in Connecticut. She picked random words from the prayer and wrote them under the vowels in a scrambled order.

"There!" she said, passing the paper to Mathilde.

Mathilde sped through the Lord's Prayer, slowed carefully to sound out the vowels, and balked when she came to the first random word at the bottom, a look of panic on her face.

"You can do it," Elizabeth encouraged her. "Sound it out and look for it above."

Mathilde clapped her hands when she found it. "It's *père*. It means *father*. I'm reading in French!"

Mathilde's excitement made Elizabeth forget the disappointment of sharing her school with Sarah Worth. Even the chill from the cold floor almost disappeared.

For the next few hours, Mathilde studied the words carefully and looked for more in her Bible, while Elizabeth read from *Robinson Crusoe*.

"I can't do anymore tonight," Mathilde said finally, rubbing her eyes. She put the paper carefully in the basket. "You keep it. If my brothers find it, they might suspect something."

"You can come over every evening and practise. I'll ask Papa if I can bring in the bearskin rug and it will be the coziest school in the world."

"There's only twelve more days until Christmas. I have an idea that will make those brothers of mine think twice before they tease me again."

Mathilde explained her idea and Elizabeth agreed that it would make Christmas Eve unforgettable for both families.

"We'll have to start right after supper tomorrow night. It's going to take a lot of work."

In the soft glow of the lantern light, Elizabeth saw her reflection in Mathilde's happy eyes. It was going to be the Brightmans' first Christmas in Nova Scotia—the best Christmas ever.

It was unfathomable how school brought out the worst in Sarah.

"Am *I* a bossy teacher?" Elizabeth asked.

They'd had three warm days in a row. Elizabeth waited with Mathilde by the barn door for Papa to bring out the sleigh. The snow was melting and there were a few puddles and brown patches on the ground. If it stayed warm another day, there'd be no more sleigh rides until the next heavy snowfall.

"Oh, no," Mathilde assured her, knowing what Elizabeth was getting at. "When God was giving out bossiness, he gave it all to Sarah Worth. Teaching makes her think she knows something that we don't."

"She's not coming today, remember."

Mathilde grinned. "I never thought I'd look forward to making soap!"

Yesterday, they'd agreed that if the thaw continued, they'd have to help Mathilde make soap for the Porters. Sarah had protested that the fumes hurt her eyes and had said that though she wouldn't come, Ginny could. A look had passed among Ginny, Elizabeth, and Mathilde, a look of relief.

Suddenly, a wet snowball thudded into the puddle in front of Mathilde, splashing water all over her skirt.

"Lucien!" Mathilde yelled.

Her older brother laughed at them from the woods. He was a tall, handsome boy with an engaging smile, and even though he was wicked to Mathilde, Elizabeth knew why Sarah liked him.

A torrent of French went back and forth between brother and sister. Mathilde's face was bright red.

Lucien scratched his head as he approached. "I don't know what you get so mad about. It's just a little water."

"I have to make soap outside all afternoon at the Porters' or the fumes will make us sick. I'm going to be cold and wet. How would you like it?"

Papa drove the sleigh out of the barn, and Lucien closed the wide door for them.

"Come on, Mathilde. I'm sorry."

Papa quickly assessed the situation—Mathilde's angry face, her wet skirt, and Lucien's guilty expression.

Papa winked at Elizabeth. "Your mother's got a hundred things for me to do this afternoon. How about if Lucien drives you today and gives you a hand with that heavy cauldron for the soap?"

Lucien rolled his eyes; a smug look spread across Mathilde's face.

"That all right with you, Lucien?" Papa asked.

"Yes, Mr. Brightman," Lucien said, stepping up to drive the sleigh.

"Girls?" Papa winked at Elizabeth.

"Yes, Mr. Brightman!" she said with Mathilde.

All the way to the Porters, they sat like queens under the bearskin rug. To Lucien's credit, he never complained once and readily helped Mr. Porter half-carry, half-roll the heavy iron cauldron out the back kitchen door to the open yard, where they hung it over a firepit. Mr. Porter nodded his usual silent thanks and was gone.

Joshua helped Lucien bring a pile of logs from the wood stack. Elizabeth got a fire going under the cauldron while Mathilde poured lye-water into it and then added lard. Ginny had brought some saved fat scraps from the Worths' house and those were stirred in too. The five of them stood around the cauldron waiting for the mixture to boil.

"Can we still have school today?" Joshua asked.

Elizabeth froze. Maybe Lucien hadn't heard.

He had. "What school is that?"

Mathilde's shoulders went high and stiff and she stopped stirring the mess in the cauldron.

Hoping to get Joshua away before he said another word, Elizabeth grabbed his hand and tugged on Ginny's sleeve. "Let's go inside and get started."

"Without Mathilde?" Joshua asked, turning back to the fire. "Aren't you learning to read today?"

Lucien hooted. "Read? Mathilde's learning to read?"

"Hush, Joshua," Ginny scolded.

It was too late. The secret was out. Elizabeth wished that Papa had come instead of Lucien, but wishing didn't change anything.

Mathilde spun around. She pointed the long stirring stick at her older brother as she hissed something at him in French.

"This is too good." Lucien laughed. "Why should I keep it a secret?"

"Because you'll spoil everything." Mathilde's eyes were filling with tears. "You'll spoil everything like you always do."

Behind them at the kitchen door a voice called, "Hello, everybody."

They all turned. Sarah Worth couldn't have picked a worse time.

"Hello, Lucien." Sarah's face softened and she smiled her sweetest smile.

"Hello, Sarah." Lucien's face changed too, and for a second Elizabeth felt like an intruder on a private moment.

"What are *you* doing here? I thought you couldn't stand the fumes," Mathilde asked.

Sarah walked toward them, lifting her skirt prettily with one hand, holding out a wooden jug to Mathilde with the other. "Mama asked why I didn't come today. When she found out you were making soap she sent me with all our candle drippings. Papa brought me in the cutter ..."

They heard a man's voice somewhere calling, "Sarah? Joshua?" and all the colour drained from Sarah's face.

Mathilde looked horrified. "Is your papa out front?"

Sarah nodded fearfully.

Elizabeth urged her quickly, "Go, Sarah. If your father comes back here and sees Lucien, there'll be so much trouble."

Sarah turned to leave … too late. Her father appeared at the back corner of the house, trudging through the soft snow. He carried his driver's whip in his hand. His eyes scanned them: Mathilde and Lucien by the fire, Elizabeth between Joshua and Ginny, and Sarah almost at the kitchen door.

His face turned red. He scowled at Sarah.

"What's that boy doing here? I told you never to see that boy again."

"I didn't know he was here, Papa."

Caleb Worth didn't seem to listen to her answer. He glared at Lucien. "Have you been seeing my daughter? Using this school as an excuse? Get over here, boy, and answer me."

Lucien didn't budge.

Ginny reached for Elizabeth's hand and squeezed it tightly. Elizabeth's heart pounded.

She remembered everything that Papa had said Caleb Worth could do to the LeBlancs if he wanted. He could have them all thrown back in prison or deported again. As Acadians, they had no rights in Nova Scotia.

The long, thin end of the whip hung loose from Caleb Worth's hand. It hung like a threat on the white snow. Did he mean to use it on Lucien?

Mathilde dropped the stirring stick and ran before Caleb Worth. She knelt in the wet snow and put her hands together, pleading, "Please, sir. My brother only came today to help me make soap. We weren't expecting Sarah to be here. Mr. Brightman couldn't come and he ordered Lucien to help me with the heavy cauldron. You can ask Mr. Brightman yourself, sir. It's been me and Joshua and Ginny learning to read here. Never Lucien, sir."

Caleb Worth glowered at them all. "Get in the cutter, Sarah. We're paying a little visit to the Brightmans. Now."

He turned and was gone, the whip dragging

like the tail of the devil himself. Sarah was forced to run behind, her skirts hiked up awkwardly, her face flushed with emotion.

No one moved until they heard the faint crack of the whip in the air and they knew that Caleb Worth had left. Elizabeth felt Joshua tug on her other hand.

"Doesn't Uncle Caleb like Lucien?" Joshua looked lost and upset.

Ginny let go of Elizabeth's hand. She reached out her arms and picked up Joshua. She swung him playfully back and forth until he smiled. "Don' pay no mind to your Uncle Caleb. He just don' know Lucien like a body should."

Mathilde put her hands in the snow and pushed herself back to her feet. Head down, she turned and walked unsteadily back to the fire. Lucien reached out a hand to stop her, and Elizabeth heard him say, *"Merci, ma soeur."*

Mathilde fell against him, sobbing, and he wrapped his arms around her, talking to her softly in French.

She knelt in the wet snow and put her hands together, pleading, "Please, sir. My brother only came today to help me make soap."

Elizabeth looked away. She'd never imagined that Mathilde and Lucien could be close like that. She remembered the LeBlancs' stories about the hardships they'd faced after the deportation and how badly people had treated them in Massachusetts.

Elizabeth feared Caleb Worth more than ever. She turned to Ginny. What was it like to be a slave in his house? It was almost too horrible to ask. "Has he ever … do you think … was he going to use that whip on Lucien?"

Ginny shook her head vehemently. "Master Worth? He be full o' rules and a fright to look at when he's mad, but no, I never knowed him to use a whip 'cept in his carriage."

Elizabeth pondered this information. Maybe she'd made too hasty a judgment about Sarah's father. But he was so different from *her* papa. Caleb Worth's face turned a fearsome red when he was angry and he glowered and thundered, but … was he maybe like a barking dog? All bark and no bite? It was all too hard to fathom. She put Caleb Worth out of her mind. But the way Mathilde had stuck up for her brother—that was something Elizabeth would never forget.

Ginny smiled at her and motioned with her head to the open back door. "If this be my one day to have you as my teacher, I wish we'd get started."

CHAPTER N.º 9

Before they started their lessons the next day, Ginny told Elizabeth and Mathilde, word for word, what had transpired at the Worths' supper table. Joshua and his father had been invited. Joshua had immediately asked, "Is Sarah still in trouble?" Caleb Worth had tried to shush him, but Joshua had persisted. "Uncle Caleb, were you going to whip Lucien?" Then Mistress Worth had insisted on knowing the meaning of Joshua's questions. Master Worth had to explain everything. Mr. Brightman had convinced him that Lucien had not gone to the Porters' with any expectation of meeting Sarah. Mr. Porter had spoken up, commenting on Lucien's kindness in accompanying his sister and Elizabeth to help with the soap-making. Supper had ended badly. Mistress Worth had left the table, claiming that her husband was frightening women and children to death.

"Uncle Caleb sleepin' on the sofa again," Ginny said. "And your cousin Sarah's forbidden comin' here while there's school with Acadians." Ginny shook her head with exaggerated sadness and poked Joshua. "A crying shame. We won' get your cousin Sarah as a teacher no more."

With the honesty of a five-year-old, Joshua replied, "That's the only good thing. Cousin Sarah was too bossy. I like Elizabeth better."

How quickly the tables could turn! Joshua's words warmed Elizabeth's heart. She had her students back! Her school! But her next thought was for Sarah. Poor Sarah, stuck at home with her parents fighting again. She didn't feel one drop of pity for Caleb Worth. She hoped he stayed on the sofa for a long time.

"What about your secret?" Elizabeth asked Mathilde, as she handed out hornbooks and slate boards.

"Lucien and I came to an agreement. He won't say a word or spoil our surprise for Christmas Eve."

"A surprise?" Joshua asked eagerly.

"And it's a *secret*." Mathilde poked him. "But you can be part of it, if your papa says you can come. We'll ask him when he gets home. We're going to show the Brightmans how Acadians celebrate Christmas Eve. You get to stay up all night and eat and sing and dance. Would your parents mind more guests, Elizabeth?"

Mind? Elizabeth knew her parents would squeeze the whole community into their small parlour if they could. The joy of Christmas was best shared with others. With a pang of sadness, Elizabeth considered Sarah. She'd never be allowed to enjoy an Acadian Christmas Eve, especially one with Lucien LeBlanc. No. Asking would only cause more trouble, and there was already too much strife at the Worths' house.

"They love visitors," Elizabeth said, turning hopefully to Ginny. "You can be part of it, if you like. And maybe your mama, too? If you think you'd be free to join us?"

Ginny smiled wryly. "Free? We still prayin' for that. But I'll ask Master Worth if he'd mind our steppin' out a spell."

CHAPTER N.º 10

The morning before Christmas, Elizabeth woke up hoping to see snowflakes. Something white pressed against the window, but it wasn't snow.

Elizabeth ran down the stairs and flung open the front door. She couldn't see the barn or the LeBlancs' house or a tree anywhere. The world had disappeared. They were lost in a thick cloud of heavy fog.

"I can't see a thing!" she wailed. Mama and Papa rushed from the kitchen.

"What's wrong?"

She pointed. "How will anyone get here tonight? How will we have Christmas Eve? How will Mathilde and I ..."

She stopped just in time. She and Mathilde had worked so hard, Elizabeth didn't want to spoil the secret now.

Papa laughed. "I've already been to the barn and brought back a goose for dinner tomorrow. See that rope?"

Elizabeth hadn't noticed the rope leading from the front door, across the ground, and into the white mist.

"And Joseph did the same thing from his house. We met in the barn while sleepyheads were dreaming. You didn't want to help me kill the goose, did you?"

Even though Papa was teasing, Elizabeth shook her head violently. She hated killing chickens and animals from the barn.

"If you yell good and loud, I expect Mathilde will answer," Papa suggested.

Elizabeth stepped outside and turned in what

she thought was the direction of Mathilde's house.

She put her hands around her mouth and called, "Mathilde?" It felt strange to call into the void.

She waited. Ahead in the fog she heard a door creak open, then—

"Elizabeth?"

Elizabeth laughed. She couldn't see Mathilde but she could hear her. "Can you meet me in the barn? I have to do my chores and then we can …" Was the whole world listening? "You know what."

"In a minute. I'll get my things."

Elizabeth got her basket and a lantern. "I'll be back later to help pluck the goose. Mama, can you come with us for a few minutes?"

"You girls are up to something," Papa said, a question on his face.

"Maybe. Maybe not," Elizabeth said, giving him a reassuring kiss. "If we are, you'll find out tonight."

Sworn to secrecy, Mama came out to the barn to rehearse her part and then left. The morning flew by. A ray of sunshine appeared through a crack in the barn wall.

"The fog's lifted!" Elizabeth said happily.

They separated for the afternoon, each needing to prepare for the evening. The goose was plucked and put in the cold cellar. It would be roasted tomorrow for Christmas dinner. Elizabeth had found fresh cranberries near a little marsh. Most she cooked with sugar, but a few she tied around cedar boughs that she placed in the parlour. She put fresh hay in the baby's cradle by the hearth and a rocking chair beside it.

"You've made it so cheerful and welcoming," Mama exclaimed, standing next to Elizabeth and admiring the parlour. She had one hand under her belly as if to help hold the baby within.

"Do you think the others will come?"

Mama looked at the cradle. "Visitors came for the real birth. From far away, just following a star and a story."

Elizabeth smiled. "It will be a Christmas of surprises."

Elizabeth hummed and skipped around the house. After supper she and Mama lit candles in the front windows and more lanterns than usual to brighten the parlour, where the fire roared. The smell of cinnamon from a pot of mulled cider filled the whole house, and that was the first thing the LeBlancs noticed when they finally arrived.

"It smells like heaven in here!" Joseph LeBlanc said.

Mathilde nodded, pushing ahead of her three tall brothers. They all looked like Lucien, although the eldest, Sebastien, had tight curls that hung in thick locks past his ears.

"We could smell cinnamon all the way from our house!" Mathilde carried a dish of something wrapped in a cloth. So did her mother. "We've been baking all day for this."

Mama led them to the kitchen, where the table was now covered in food for the midnight feast. Then they joined the menfolk in the parlour for a drink of cider, but Papa was greeting someone else at the front door.

To Elizabeth's delight, she saw Mr. Porter and little Joshua. About ten feet behind them, Ginny stood in the shadows with her mother. Both looked uncertain.

Elizabeth ushered the Porters into the house while Papa called to Ginny and her mother, "Come in and join us."

They moved forward into the light. Ginny's mother walked stiffly and she leaned on Ginny's shoulder. Elizabeth held out a hand. "Welcome! Merry Christmas!"

Ginny's mother held out something covered in a checkered cloth. She nudged Ginny, who held out what she was carrying. "We brung y'all chicken an' cornmeal bread," her mother said with a much stronger drawl than Ginny's.

"How kind of you! You must tell me how you made them. Come in," Elizabeth's mother said, taking Ginny's offering.

Their mothers walked ahead with the food and Elizabeth led Ginny into the parlour, whispering, "Are you ready?"

Ginny nodded and they took their places beside Mathilde at the hearth, waiting for the adults to greet each other and finish sharing news.

It took too long. Mathilde kept poking her, impatient to get things started, but the three mothers were deep in a conversation. They could talk for days. Elizabeth took the family Bible from its place on the hearth and gave it to her father.

"It's going to be New Year's if we don't start soon."

Papa laughed and held up the Bible. Everyone paid attention. "Welcome to our first Christmas in Nova Scotia. Of course, it's not the LeBlancs' first Noël here"—he said the French word carefully, exactly as Mathilde had instructed—"but it's our first one together. In honour of the occasion, the girls have something prepared for us."

He gave the Bible back to Elizabeth. She found the place she'd marked so carefully on the fine, smooth pages.

She cleared her throat. "Excuse me," she said. "Ginny will begin the reading from Luke 2."

Ginny took the Bible and slowly read out the first verses of the Christmas story. "And it came to pass …"

She used the fescue, carefully pointing to each word, relying partly on her new skills, partly on her memory, to read the verses. Her mother's eyes were bright with pride. When Ginny got to the part about Mary and Joseph she stopped and passed the fescue to Mathilde.

Mathilde opened her family Bible while Ginny introduced her. "Mathilde's gonna read the next part about Bethlehem in French. Don' worry none if you don' understand. Jess watch Mary an' Joseph. Here they come."

On cue, Mama and Joshua walked slowly from the hallway toward the hearth. Mama made a perfect Mary, very pregnant, and using Joshua's shoulder for support, though Joshua was only five and very small. Joshua's face shone with the importance of the role given to him. When Mama sat in the rocking chair by the empty cradle, Joshua took off his robe and held it in front of her. He took it away again, and there was a baby doll lying in the cradle.

While Mathilde read, Elizabeth peeked at the LeBlancs' faces. Mathilde's mother's eyes filled with tears and her father's looked misty too. Her brothers, even Lucien, looked as if they'd seen a ghost. Elizabeth hoped that Mathilde had gotten a glimpse of how shocked they were.

Joshua held a paper star on the end of a stick over the cradle. Elizabeth read the last few verses in English and the scene was almost over. She handed a piece of paper and the fescue to Joshua. He read out very slowly: "Glory to God in the highest, and on earth peace, good will toward men."

All the parents started talking at once.

"I didn't know she could read!"

"Who's been teaching them?"

Mathilde's brothers couldn't get over what their little sister had accomplished. "How did you do that? We want to learn to read too!"

"Maybe Elizabeth can teach *toute la famille.* All

of us," Mr. LeBlanc said, still shaking his head at the surprise of it.

Mr. Porter came up shyly to Elizabeth, Joshua's hand in his. For once, he didn't just nod at her. "Thank you, Elizabeth Brightman."

Just those four words let Elizabeth know that she'd given him a very special gift. It felt good. She caught Mama staring at her.

"I know your school is successful just the way it is," her mother said, "but if you want to hold it at our house, I could get Mathilde's mother and brothers started before the baby comes in March. That is ... if you need help."

Elizabeth turned to Ginny and Mathilde. "What do you think?"

Mathilde turned to Mr. Porter. "It's up to you, sir. Could I bring Joshua here for school, then come back to do chores?"

Mr. Porter thought about this for a minute. "Don't see why not. I'll bring Joshua and Ginny on my way to work."

Elizabeth smiled. Would wonders never cease?

While Mathilde read, Elizabeth
peeked at the LeBlancs' faces.
Mathilde's mother's eyes filled with
tears and her father's looked misty too.

Her school was growing. Now that she'd proven herself to be a teacher, she'd be happy to work with Mama. Their kitchen would be bustling with people and stories. Winter would fly by until the very best surprise of all: the new baby. The New Year promised to be full of wonderful things.

Dear Reader,

Welcome back to Our Canadian Girl! In addition to this story about Elizabeth, there are many more adventures of other spirited girls to come.

So please keep on reading. And do stay in touch. You can also log on to our website at www.ourcanadiangirl.ca and enjoy fun activities, sample chapters, a fan club, and monthly contests.

Sincerely,
 Barbara Berson
 Editor

1608
Samuel de Champlain establishes the first fortified trading post at Quebec.

1759
The British defeat the French in the Battle of the Plains of Abraham.

1812
The United States declares war against Canada.

1845
The expedition of Sir John Franklin to the Arctic ends when the ship is frozen in the pack ice; the fate of its crew remains a mystery.

1869
Louis Riel leads his Metis followers in the Red River Rebellion.

1871
British Columbia joins Canada.

1755
The British expel the entire French population of Acadia (today's Maritime provinces), sending them into exile.

1776
The 13 Colonies revolt against Britain, and the Loyalists flee to Canada.

1837
Calling for responsible government, the Patriotes, following Louis-Joseph Papineau, rebel in Lower Canada; William Lyon Mackenzie leads the uprising in Upper Canada.

1867
New Brunswick, Nova Scotia, and the United Province of Canada come together in Confederation to form the Dominion of Canada.

1870
Manitoba joins Canada. The Northwest Territories become an official territory of Canada.

1762
Elizabeth

Timeline

1885
At Craigellachie, British Columbia, the last spike is driven to complete the building of the Canadian Pacific Railway.

1898
The Yukon Territory becomes an official territory of Canada.

1914
Britain declares war on Germany, and Canada, because of its ties to Britain, is at war too.

1918
As a result of the Wartime Elections Act, the women of Canada are given the right to vote in federal elections.

1945
World War II ends conclusively with the dropping of atomic bombs on Hiroshima and Nagasaki.

1873
Prince Edward Island joins Canada.

1896
Gold is discovered on Bonanza Creek, a tributary of the Klondike River.

1905
Alberta and Saskatchewan join Canada.

1917
In the Halifax harbour, two ships collide, causing an explosion that leaves more than 1,600 dead and 9,000 injured.

1939
Canada declares war on Germany seven days after war is declared by Britain and France.

1949
Newfoundland, under the leadership of Joey Smallwood, joins Canada.

1897
Emily

1885
Marie-Claire

1940
Ellen

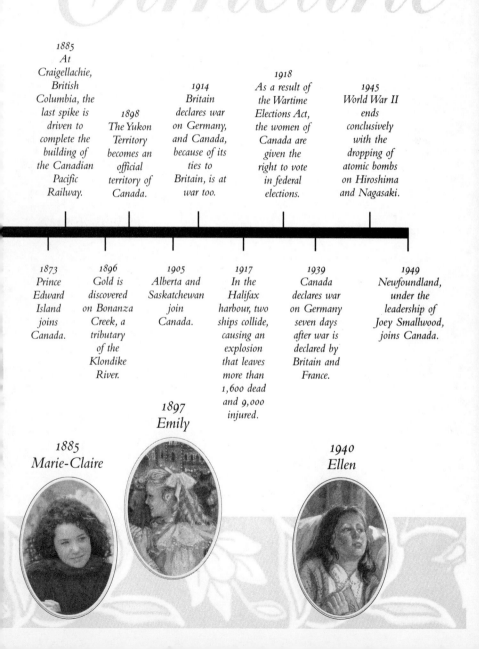